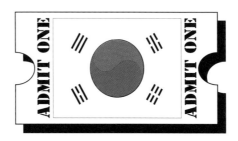

Kyongbokkung
Palace In
Seoul

FACES AND PLACES

SOUTH KOREA

BY PATRICK RYAN

THE CHILD'S WORLD®, INC.

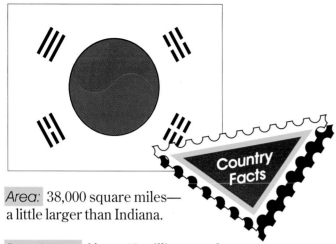

Country Facts

Area: 38,000 square miles— a little larger than Indiana.

Population: About 45 million people.

Capital City: Seoul.

Other Important Cities: Pusan, Taegu, Inchon, Kwangju, Taejon.

Money: The won.

National Language: Korean.

National Song: "The National Anthem."

National Holiday: Independence Day on August 15.

National Flag: White with black bars and a circle of red and blue in the middle. The white stands for purity. The red and blue stand for cooperation and togetherness. The black bars stand for things such as the four seasons and the four directions.

Chief of State: President Kim Dae–jung.

Text copyright © 1999 by The Child's World®, Inc.
All rights reserved. No part of this book may be reproduced or utilized in any form or by any means without written permission from the publisher.
Printed in the United States of America.

Library of Congress Cataloging-in-Publication Data
Ryan, Pat (Patrick M.)
South Korea / by Patrick Ryan
Series: "Faces and Places".
p. cm.
Includes index.
Summary: Describes the history, geography, people and customs of this peninsular Asian country.
ISBN 1-56766-517-9 (library : reinforced : alk. paper)

1. Korea (South) — Juvenile literature.
2. Korea (South) — Civilization — Juvenile literature.
[1. Korea (South)] I. Title.

DS902.R96 1998
915.195 — dc21
97-50299
CIP
AC

GRAPHIC DESIGN
Robert A. Honey, Seattle

PHOTO RESEARCH
James R. Rothaus / James R. Rothaus & Associates

ELECTRONIC PRE–PRESS PRODUCTION
Robert E. Bonaker / Graphic Design & Consulting Co.

PHOTOGRAPHY
Cover photo: Korean Boy at Folk Dance Competition by Stephanie Maze/Corbis

Table of Contents

ADMIT ONE ADMIT ONE

Earth is a big place. It has huge oceans and cold ice caps. It also has large land areas called **continents**. Some continents are made up of many different countries. South Korea is a country on the continent of Asia. South Korea is part of a land area called a **peninsula**. A peninsula has water almost all of the way around it. South Korea shares its peninsula with the country of North Korea.

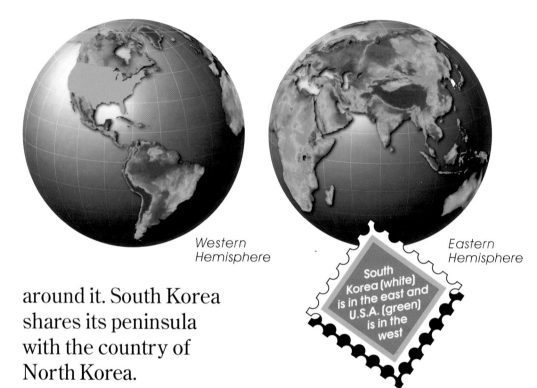

Western Hemisphere

Eastern Hemisphere

South Korea (white) is in the east and U.S.A. (green) is in the west

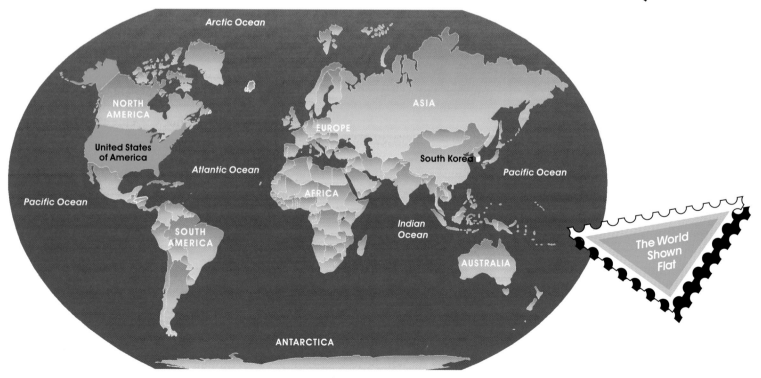

Arctic Ocean

NORTH AMERICA

United States of America

Atlantic Ocean

Pacific Ocean

ASIA

EUROPE

South Korea

Pacific Ocean

AFRICA

Indian Ocean

SOUTH AMERICA

AUSTRALIA

ANTARCTICA

The World Shown Flat

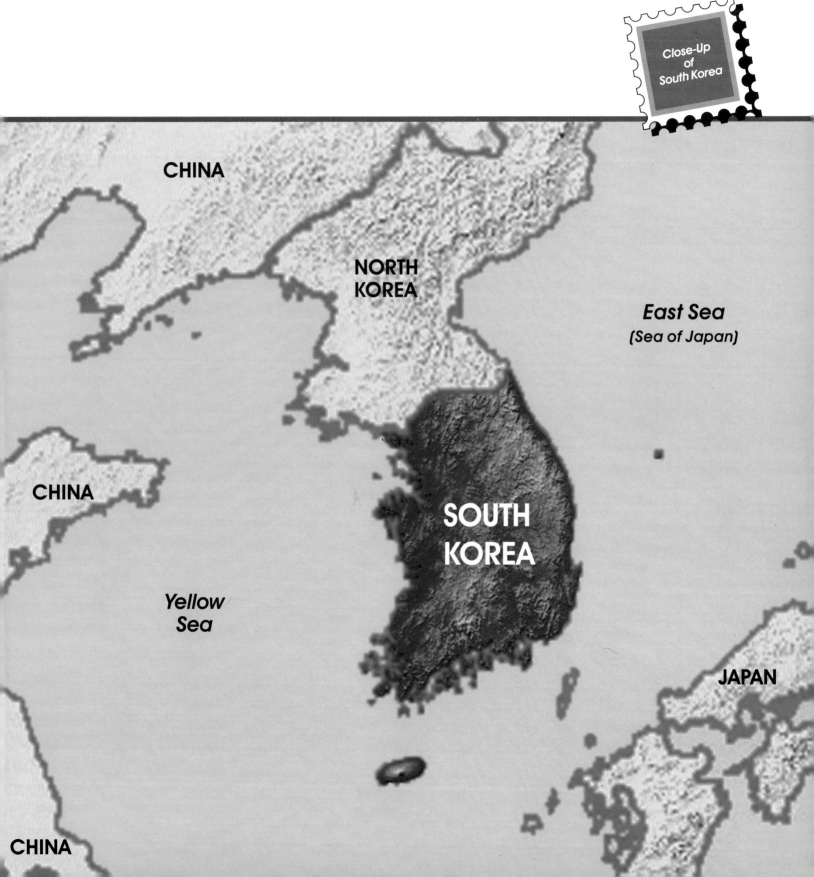

CHINA

Close-Up
of
South Korea

CHINA

NORTH
KOREA

East Sea
(Sea of Japan)

CHINA

*Yellow
Sea*

SOUTH
KOREA

JAPAN

CHINA

Mount
Sorak–san
In The
Fall

Mount Sorak-san
Seoul ☆   • Kangnung
Kangwon-Do

CHEJU-DO

Corel Galleria™

The Land

South Korea has many mountains and hills. Most of them are covered with thick, green forests. There are pretty rivers that flow through the countryside, too. Besides the mountains, South Korea also has wide, flat plains. These flat areas are perfect for farming. Many **islands** can be found near South Korea's coasts. Islands are land areas that are surrounded by water on all sides. Most of South Korea's islands have no people living on them.

Farming Plain In Kangwon-Do

Corel Galleria™

Chonjiyon Waterfall On Cheju-Do Island

Wolfgang Kaehler/Corbis

Dawn Near Kangnung

Kevin R. Morris/Corbis

South Korea's forests are full of life. Trees such as maple, elm, and fir all grow tall and green. Bamboo trees and other tropical plants live in many areas, too. The thick woods hide many shy animals such as deer and mice. Bears, wild pigs, and many kinds of birds also live there. And the deep ocean waters near South Korea's shore are home to all kinds of fish and other water creatures.

Michael Callan; Frank Lane Picture Agency/Corbis

Roe Deer On Cheju–Do Island

Oxen Are Used In Kyongsan Rice Paddies

Corel Galleria™

Corel Galleria™

Kyongsan • Songma

CHEJU-DO

Pine Tree
Grows
Near
Songma

Hall Of Kyungbok
Royal Palace
In Seoul

☆Seoul

Kyongju •

Wolfgang Kaehler/Corbis

South Korea and North Korea used to be one country. It was simply called *Korea*.
Long ago, Korea was made up of many small kingdoms. Over time, the little kingdoms joined together. They formed three large kingdoms called *Koguryo, Paekche,* and *Silla*. The Silla kingdom ruled Korea for 200 years.

Leonard de Selva/Corbis

Japanese Occupation Of Seoul In 1904

As the years passed, many other groups ruled Korea—even the country of Japan. Japan fought in World War II and was defeated. When the war was over, Korea was split into two countries. North Korea and South Korea were given their own names and their own governments. But both sides were unhappy. They both wanted to control all of Korea.

Pulguksa Temple In Kyongju

Carmen Redondo/Corbis

Carmen Redondo/Corbis

8th Century Sokkuram Shrine In Kyongju

Guarding The DMZ Fence

As the two Koreas tried to reunite their country, fighting began. People from the North began attacking people from the South. This conflict was called the *Korean War*. After three years of fighting, both sides agreed to stop.

Today Koreans are working for peace. The two governments try to settle their differences. They have signed agreements to stop fighting, too. But working for peace can be very difficult. Sometimes South Koreans are afraid war will return.

City Hall In Seoul

Kevin R. Morris/Corbis

The 1950 Invasion Of Inchon By US Troops

Jim Sugar Photography/Corbis

Hulton–Deutsch Collection/Corbis

Kevin R. Morris/Corbis

DMZ

Inchon ● ☆ Seoul

Downtown
Seoul
Today

LOTTE LOTTE

Newcomer's
View Of
Seoul

☆ Seoul   • Kangnung

Kyongju •
Pusan •

About 45 million people live in South Korea. Most of them are native Koreans. Over the years, many **immigrants**, or newcomers from other countries, have been coming to South Korea, too. They are looking for good jobs and places to live. Most of South Korea's immigrants come from the country of China.

Girls Having Fun In Kangnung

Kevin R. Morris/Corbis

Modern Day Pusan Foot Traffic

Buddhist Man From Kyongju

Kevin R. Morris/Corbis

Kevin R. Morris/Corbis

17

ADMIT ONE

City Life
And
Country
Life

ADMIT ONE

Apartments
In
Seoul

Kevin R. Morris/Corbis

Most South Koreans live in cities. They own apartments or small houses and work in offices, stores, and factories. South Korean cities have fast cars, crowded streets, and subway systems just like those in the United States. Some South Korean cities are very large, too. Seoul, the capital city, has about 10 million people. South Korea's country people live differently.

Michael S. Yamashita/Corbis

Instead of tall apartment buildings, they live in simple houses made from bricks. They work on the land or the sea, farming or fishing until the sun goes down. Some country people also travel to the cities to work.

Colorful
Houses On
Cheju–Do
Island

Traditional
House
in
Yangdong
Village

Michael Freeman/Corbis

☆ Seoul

Yangdong
Village ●

Corel Galleria™

CHEJU-DO

People
Of Seoul
Relax On
The Han
River

Neon Signs
Mix Korean
And
Western
Alphabets

☆Seoul •Kangnung

Pusan

Before they start kindergarten, South Korean children attend preschools. In elementary school, they learn reading and writing just as you do. They also learn math. The alphabet in South Korea is called *hangul*. It has 24 letters. South Koreans use a few Chinese symbols when they write, too.

Kevin R. Morris/Corbis

The official language of South Korea is Korean. It is different from other languages. It is somewhat like Japanese, but has many words taken from the Chinese language, too.

Students In Playground In Pusan

College Students From Kangnung

Students Of Isabel School In Pusan

Kevin R. Morris/Corbis

Kevin R. Morris/Corbis

Work

Woman Working On Boat In Pusan

Kevin R. Morris/Corbis

Many of the products we use come from South Korea. Cars, televisions, running shoes, and clothing are just a few of the things made there. VCRs and compact disc players also come from South Korean factories. South Korea's rich farmland grows rice, sweet potatoes, corn, cotton, and wheat for the nation's people. Many people work long hours to catch fish with huge nets. Whatever their job is, South Koreans work very hard.

Farmer Harvesting Rice In Cholla Area

Auto Assembly Line In Pup'yong

Nathan Benn/Corbis

Nathan Benn/Corbis

☆ Seoul

Pup'yong

CHOLLA

Pusan

Kevin R. Morris/Corbis

SOGONG SHOPPING CENTER

Fresh Fruit Vendor In Pusan

Suwon

Taegu
Pusan

Kevin R. Morris/Corbis

Fish Market Workers In Pusan

Kevin R. Morris/Corbis

Rice is the most important food in South Korea. It is eaten at almost every meal. Fish, barley, peaches, beans, and sweet potatoes are important foods, too. South Koreans also like spices. One popular dish, called *kimchi* (KIM-chee), is made with cabbage, radishes, garlic, and red peppers. People make it in many different ways. Sometimes kimchi is very, VERY spicy.

Kimchi From Taegu

Suwon Woman Cooking Over Grill

Michael S. Yamashita/Corbis

Corel Galleria™

South Koreans love to have fun. They like sports such as soccer, boxing, baseball, and tennis. They also like to go to concerts, plays, and movies, just as you do. Other popular pastimes include **martial arts**. Martial arts teach people how to defend themselves. *Tae kwon do* (TY-KWAN-DOH) is a popular martial art in South Korea.

Olympic Baseball Stadium In Seoul

Janet Wishnetsky/Corbis

Suwon Villagers On Seesaw

Michael S. Yamashita/Corbis

Traditional Dance And Costumes

Michael S. Yamashita/Corbis

☆ Seoul
• Suwon

Tae Kwon Do
Competition

Corel Galleria™

☆ Seoul

Kyongju •

Dancers
Celebrating
Confucius'
Birthday
In Seoul

Traditional Korean Wedding In Kyongju

Michael Lewis/Corbis

South Koreans celebrate holidays and festivals by watching the stars and planets in the sky. In late January or early February they celebrate their New Year. People dress in their best clothes and remember their relatives of long ago. Then it is time to enjoy a big feast. South Koreans also have fun family celebrations. Weddings and birthdays are very happy times.

They are celebrated with special foods and gifts. Family members all gather to talk and laugh together on these days.

South Korea is a small country that is growing stronger every day. After many difficult years, South Koreans are working hard to keep their country peaceful and happy. Perhaps one day you will visit this beautiful land of hills and mountains. If you do, look around—and remember how hard South Koreans have worked to live in peace.

Armed Forces Day In Seoul

Janet Wishnetsky/Corbis

Did You Know?

South Korea is really called the "Republic of Korea." People just say "South Korea" for short.

About 200 years ago, Seoul was a walled city with gates that closed at night.

*South Korea's weather is caused by winds called **monsoons**. During the summer, monsoons from the south bring in hot, sticky weather. During the winter, cold, dry monsoons from the north bring cold weather.*

*South Korea has the oldest existing **observatory** in Asia. It is called Chomsongdae. This stone building stands 29 feet tall and is made up of 365 stones. It was built more than 1,000 years ago to help people look at the stars.*

How Do You Say?

	KOREAN	HOW TO SAY IT
Hello	annyong haseyo	(ahn-yong hay-sey-yoh)
Goodbye	annyong	(ahn-nyong)
Please	putakhamnida	(poo-tok-hahm-nee-dah)
Thank You	kamsahamnida	(kahm-sah-hahm-nee-dah)
One	hana	(hah-nah)
Two	tul	(tool)
Three	set	(sett)
South Korea	Nam Ham	(nam hahm)

Glossary

continents (KON-tih-nents)
Earth's huge land areas are called continents. South Korea is on the continent of Asia.

immigrants (IH-mih-grents)
Immigrants are newcomers from other countries. Many South Koreans are immigrants from China.

islands (EYE-landz)
Islands are land areas that are surrounded by water on all sides. There are many islands along South Korea's coast.

martial arts (MAR-shull ARTS)
Martial arts are activities that teach people how to defend themselves. Many South Koreans practice martial arts.

monsoons (mon-SOONZ)
Monsoons are winds that change South Korea's weather. Summer monsoons are hot and wet, and winter monsoons are cold and dry.

observatory (ob-ZER-vuh-toh-ree)
An observatory is a place where people go to study the stars. South Korea has one of the oldest observatories in the world.

peninsula (puh-NIN-soo-luh)
A peninsula is a land area that has water most of the way around it. South Korea lies on a peninsula that is attached to the continent of Asia.

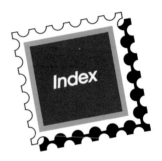

Index